DAMAGE CONTROL

SKYE WARREN

CHAPTER ONE
Eva Morelli

THE OFFENDING DESSERTS steam from the counter. Two thousand miniature mince pies line up in neat rows. My mother stares at them as if they spit on her heritage.

I pick one up, flaky pastry warm between my fingertips. A delicious mixture of currants and apples blooms on my tongue. A candied orange peel on top provides a pleasant bite.

"It tastes good," I say, knowing that won't matter.

"Nutmeg," my mother says with haughty indignance. "There isn't nearly enough. It's mostly cinnamon."

Sarah Morelli may have married an Italian man, but her family came over on the Mayflower.

Along with this recipe for mince pies.

She won't let anyone forget it, even if it means throwing away two thousand canapés.

"I'll fix this," I say with more confidence than

I feel.

She doesn't ask how. She just gives me a serene smile. "I can always count on you, Eva."

The Morelli galas are legendary in Bishop's Landing. If we don't serve these, my mother will hear about it for months at the high-society committee meetings she attends.

"I should get back out there," she says. "Or they'll ask after me."

I obediently kiss my mother's cheek when she turns to the side. She's the host of this event. But I'm the one who works with the caterers, the decorators, the waitstaff.

Every single person in a white dress shirt and black pants has a job tonight. They bustle efficiently through the large service kitchen, dropping off empty glasses of champagne and leaving with fresh trays of canapés. I can't take them off their current jobs—and besides, this is too important to pass to someone else. I'll need to fix the mince pies myself.

Whipped cream, I decide. With plenty of nutmeg. I can pipe it into a neat swirl on top of the pies. No one will even know they were altered from how the caterer made them.

"What's wrong?" My younger sister Daphne looks grown up in a black sheath dress. Her expression, however, is anxious. Sarah Morelli has that impact on us. We may be adults now, but we still obey our mother.

"The mince pies. I need to make about two tons of whipped cream for them."

She makes a face. "I'll help you."

"No, go back out there. The more of us missing, the more people will notice." I'm already pulling out jugs of whole milk from the industrial sized fridge.

"Ugh, if only I knew how to make whipped cream."

Neither of us really enjoy the formal events our parents host, but we're both used to them. The fake smiles. The drunken laughter. "If it were a kind of paint, you could make it."

"Or a color." She eyes the mince pies dubiously. "That shade of brown is not inspiring."

She's always preferred chocolate desserts. "Besides, this is the first Morelli gala that has Constantines. I need someone standing guard in case trouble breaks out."

A snort. "What would I do if trouble broke out?"

The Constantines have been our family's archenemy forever. None of us know exactly how it started except our parents, and they aren't talking.

Then my brother Leo fell in love with Haley Constantine.

For that reason we extended an invitation to a few of her family members. Reluctantly. Begrudgingly. And we've been tense the entire time, wondering if something will go wrong. A verbal altercation would be bad. A physical altercation would be worse.

Even between high-society billionaires, violence is common enough.

"Pretend to faint," I advise. "Someone will have to call an ambulance."

"More likely I'd get trampled."

"You're right. If anything sketchy happens, come get me." I locate a large bottle of nutmeg. If this were the family kitchen upstairs I'd be lucky to find a half-empty jar of dried spices, but we're downstairs where the staff works so it's fully stocked. "I'll be done here soon, and I'll come out."

She sighs. "I'll make sure Sophie isn't bothering Mom."

We're the good daughters, according to our mother.

Lisbetta is at her boarding school in Switzerland to keep her out of trouble. And Sophia—

well, Sophie has always been contrary. If you say go right, she goes left. The dress code for the gala was formalwear in black, white, gold, and red.

Naturally Sophie showed up in clashing hot pink.

After Daphne goes upstairs, I pull out a professional stand mixer.

In minutes I'm covered in sugar and stray flecks of whipped cream. At least they don't show up against the black and white lace covering my floor-length gown.

I use a spatula to move the mixture into a piping bag.

Footsteps approach me from behind. They're not the soft tap of my sister's heels. Or the whisper of my mother's gown against the floor. They're the hard, sure steps of a man.

"Don't bother talking me out of it," I say to my brother Leo. He doesn't understand why I work so hard to keep our mother happy, and he's probably here to drag me upstairs.

"I would never dream of it," comes a low, masculine rumble.

I whirl in surprise, sending sprays of white cream across crisp black dress pants. The man wearing them is handsome, well-built, and, unfortunately, amused at my expense. "Oh my god," I breathe.

"Don't tell me they have you slaving away in the kitchen? That's grim, even for a Morelli." Finn Hughes leans back against a counter and crosses his arms, unconcerned with the whipped cream that's setting into what's no doubt a ten-thousand-dollar bespoke tuxedo.

I grab a dish towel and bend down to wipe the cream from him in fast, efficient strokes. I'm trying not to touch him inappropriately, but I can feel his heat through the fabric. His powerful thighs form a backdrop to my frantic wipes. "What are you even doing down here? This is the service kitchen."

He looks down and raises an eyebrow. "I imagined you kneeling at my feet many times, but there was never whipped cream involved. A lack of imagination on my part, to be sure."

My cheeks burn. "I can't send you back upstairs looking like this."

"Absolutely not. People would think we'd gotten up to something." His arms are still crossed, as if he's unconcerned. As if he's enjoying this. "If only they were right."

I stand and throw up my hands. "If you don't care about your tux, I don't know why I'm bothering."

He glances back at the throngs of servers. "There isn't anyone else who could help you?"

"They're busy. Besides, this is my mother's recipe. If it's not right…"

I don't have to finish the sentence. My parents aren't known for being flexible. Finn Hughes knows that. "And Eva Morelli is the good dutiful daughter."

"Go back upstairs," I say, exasperated.

He chuckles, a deep sound that presses straight between my legs.

He's from the Constantine family, strictly speaking. His mother is Caroline Constantine's sister. Geneva married into the infamous Hughes family. Which is why he's always been invited to the Gala, even before this year. My mother isn't going to snub the Vanderbilts. She isn't going to snub the Kennedys. And she's not going to snub the Hugheses—regardless of longstanding feuds.

"I'll help you," he says.

"Absolutely not." My voice sounds breathless. I have to tilt my head up to look at him. When did he get so close? We're only inches away. If I leaned forward our bodies would be touching.

"Why not?"

"Because my mother would freak out if she found you down here."

"I'll tell her I insisted," he says with his megawatt grin that has probably gotten him out of trouble more times than I can imagine. Between his irresistible charm, his gorgeous silhouette, and a massive trust fund, this is not a man who's been told no many times. "I'll tell her that I want to learn how to bake after watching the Great British Bake Off. And you're tutoring me."

He's teasing me, and I want to be stern, but I can't keep a smile from teasing my lips. If I give him actual work to do, he'll probably disappear. "Fine. You can pipe this while I make more."

"Show me how."

I lean over the counter to pipe a circle of cream in a simple design on a small mince pie. When I lean back I see that he's been checking out my backside. Heat flashes through my body. I clear my throat and hand over the piping bag, aiming for an imperious expression I've seen my mother employ. "Your turn."

His hair is brown, but his lashes gleam almost blonde against his tanned cheeks. He takes the piping bag from me and makes a clumsy circle around a mince pie. A little whipped cream ends up on the side of his hand. He meets my eyes and licks it off. I can read every dirty thought in those mischievous brown eyes. Every promise. Every position that he thinks about when he's using his tongue.

My eyes widen. I speak past the knot in my throat. "Right. You can do the rest of the pies now."

I whirl back around to face the mixer, my body alight. My nipples must be pressing against the silk lining my dress. Warmth pools between my legs. A husky laugh follows me.

I'm not sure I could speak again if my life depended on it.

I busy myself preparing another mixture. I keep my gaze straight ahead, but inside I'm listening behind me. I'm expecting to hear footsteps wander away.

Instead there's only a concentrated quiet.

Who knew that Finn Hughes would actually help me?

His swirls aren't as neat as mine, but they're passable. And he works quickly, so that by the time I'm done with this bowl he's ready for the fresh piping bag I hand him.

We cover two thousand mince pies with nutmeg cream.

Then we're standing there, surveying our work. I'm aware of his gaze on me.

He brushes his thumb across my cheek, coming away white with whipped cream.

My breath catches. I look at him, drawn by some unnamable force. Heat races across my skin, a powerful reaction to the brief caress. It sounds insane, but I want him to touch me again.

"Eva," he murmurs.

I shake my head. "We can't."

I'm not sure what I'm refusing. A kiss. A fuck. I'm refusing to have anything to do with handsome men who murmur promises that I'm weak enough to believe.

His lips quirk. "I could make you enjoy it."

"That's even worse."

A soft laugh. Then his hand lifts my chin. My eyes fall closed. Warm lips descend on mine. I gasp at the contact, and he presses the advantage, opening me, invading me.

He pulls me flush against his hard body, and I feel the ridge of his erection against my stomach. Instinct makes me pull away, but he holds me— firm and unconcerned. "We have to stop."

His lips brush the curve of my ear. "I could sit you on this counter and drag your dress up. I could taste your pussy. Would it taste like nutmeg? Would it be sweet like whipped cream? No, you'll have your own perfect flavor. The staff would watch, but they wouldn't stop me."

"My mother—"

"She wouldn't stop me, either. No, she'd be happy enough to land a Hughes. Your father would sell you to me as if you were a plump calf on his farm. How much would you cost, do you think?"

I squirm away from him, but I'm trapped between his hard body and the counter. "I'm not an animal."

A grunt escapes him. He holds tight on my hips. "Don't move, darling. Not unless you want to be on your back, your ankles locked behind my back."

His erection flexes against my hip—a subtle threat. I go still.

He teases my earlobe gently between his teeth. "You act like the quiet, dutiful daughter, but I think you're more than that. You have secrets, Eva Morelli. And I'm going to know them."

A shiver runs through me. He sounds sure. "Never."

"And once I know them, you'll do anything to keep me from telling the rest of the world, won't you? I'll be able to do anything to you as the price for my silence."

I stiffen. "That's blackmail."

He presses a gentle kiss to my temple. "Precisely."

Then he steps back. I'm sucking in a breath, grasping the counter for balance. He disappears in a blur of expensive linen and wool. God, I'm in way over my head with him.

Then again, his threat was probably empty. There are a hundred beautiful young women upstairs. Many of them would be willing to go into a dark alcove with him tonight. Despite the religious reason for the season, there are always hookups that happen at the gala.

The thought of him with another woman makes my stomach drop.

Which is ridiculous.

I have no claim on him. And more importantly, he has no claim on me.

No man will ever have power over me. Not again.

CHAPTER TWO

Finn Hughes

I KEEP TO the fringes of the gala, watching women in gold and black and red. The occasional pink dress. They're all beautiful, but there's only one woman I want.

Eva Morelli. She glides through the crowd, bestowing smiles on drunk old men and stuffy old women, greeting each person by name, asking after some baby or wedding or retirement.

Even packed with chocolate fountains, the ballroom easily fits five hundred people. Most of them mingle with champagne. Others dance to a bluesy song crooned by a guy in a white suit. He used to be famous—a few decades ago. Now he probably ekes out a decent living on the private circuit, flashing those veneers to the country club set. Maybe he even makes extra by going home with a rich, lonely widow.

A few women—and a few men—look more than willing to pay.

Outside there's an eight-thousand-square-foot tent with a lobster buffet.

My whole life I've attended parties like this one. Extravagant. Over the top.

It's as ordinary to me as a family barbeque would be for someone else.

The fact that Constantines are invited this year... that's new, but it's not surprising. Those two families are obsessed with each other. They may pretend they're getting along for the sake of Leo and Lucian, but the truth is they're keeping their enemies close.

Doesn't matter. The Hughes have always been above that, even though Caroline Constantine is my aunt. My father came from oil money in Dallas. We've always been welcome at the Morelli galas. Sarah Morelli, in particular, loves me. I catch sight of her stark black dress through the crowd. She murmurs something to Eva, who scurries off to do her bidding.

I don't like it.

I don't like the way she's ordered around and overlooked, but it's not up to me, is it? However people treat Eva Morelli is no business of mine.

There's a dark presence behind me. I don't move, not even when I realize who it is. Especially when I realize who it is. It's not good to show weakness to Leo Morelli. The Hughes name and status mean nothing to a man with a legendary temper.

"Don't." That's all he says.

I could pretend I wasn't ogling his sister, but that would just waste time. "A man can look."

"No. He can't. I know my mother thinks the sun rises at the Hughes' French chateau, but I don't give a fuck. If you touch her, if you speak to her, if you so much as glance at her, I'll throw you off the Morelli estate with my bare hands."

That makes me smile. It's a slow, lazy kind of smile. It's not good to show weakness, but then again, I don't have any. "I've got a sister myself. I suppose protectiveness comes with the territory. Still, don't you think this whole growling caveman thing is a little much?"

"You don't want to press me, Hughes."

We grew up running wild amid the satin, glittering trappings of events like this one. There was one time we conspired to let loose my brother's pet gerbils in a costume party. Another time we loaded our nerf guns with the sticky-sweet profiteroles intended for dessert. We've been both friends and enemies. "You have a reputation for your temper. People believe what you feed them, but I know the real Leo Morelli. I know who gathered up the gerbils and put them back in their cage when your father wanted to drown them in the grotto."

"The gerbil wasn't salivating while looking at my sister."

I laugh without a sound. "Salivating? That's unfortunate. One does hate to be obvious."

"She's not like your other women."

"My harem, you mean? Hadn't realized you'd met them."

"I'm serious."

I turn a narrowed gaze on him, on his dark eyes and coal-black hair, on the cold countenance that holds so many secrets. Her secrets. "She's not like the other women here, who glide through the room, secure in their position and privilege. She's running around like a goddamn servant, and I don't see you doing anything to stop it."

"What happens in our family is none of your business." He pushes past me, bumping me as he goes. A crude message, but an effective one. "Hunt elsewhere, Hughes."

And I try.

I've partied with many of the young women in the crowd. Fucked them. Had threesomes with a handful of them. But there's always a fresh crop of them—ones who are finally old enough to warrant their own invitations. Ones whose families just made enough money to join this elite sphere. Nouveau riche, my aunt would say with a sniff of her large nose. Ones who've gotten back from some commune in Amsterdam or college in Switzerland.

I could *hunt*, as Leo Morelli put it, and take home delicious prey.

A woman presses herself against me. I turn to see a bubbly, blonde Patricia beaming up at me. "Finn! I've missed you." She throws her arms around me, pressing her breasts against my tux, encompassing me in a cloud of Yves Saint Laurent Black Opium. "Where have you been?"

"Working," I say, which is ironically the truth.

Connor laughs, because he's never worked a day in his life. He's on again, off again with Patricia. Judging from the way he drapes an arm over her bare shoulders, they're currently on. "We just got back from Vail. Everyone was there. Where the fuck were you?"

A stern-looking matron turns to give us a dirty look for bad language. I wink at her, and she turns back, her cheeks slightly pinker.

"Chamonix Mont Blanc has the better runs," I say, because they'll assume I was skiing and getting wasted and fucking my way through the resorts there.

"Yeah," he says, laughing his frat boy laugh. Did he practice it in the mirror or did it just come naturally to him? "A Hughes can probably reserve the black diamond runs all to himself."

Patricia takes my hand and tugs me closer. Too close. "Are you coming to the after party? A friend has the hook up at this new club. G-Eazy's supposed to be there."

"Does anyone still care about him after Halsey broke up with him?"

A giggle. She pulls me closer. It would be awkward in front of any other boyfriend. Considering how often Connor's cheated on her, it's merely exasperating. "And then after we could get high. Connor booked us a suite. Some of us are going to hang out."

I've been to my share of after parties. Someone's always got the hook up at a club, especially when we can slip them a fold of hundred dollar bills. From the look in Patricia's eyes, she wants to get up close and personal tonight. I've fucked her. And, separately, I've fucked Connor. Don't judge. Repressed frat boys can be a great ride. Maybe if I fucked them together?

When you've done everything, it's hard to

find something new.

It doesn't matter how beautiful they are, or how talented their mouths. I don't want the people standing in front of me. I'm not even sure I want sex.

Instead I want the secrets held in sad, dark eyes.

"Text me later," I say, extricating myself from Patricia's grip.

Screw Vail and G-Eazy. Screw Leo Morelli.

I want Eva.

That turns out to be a more difficult task than expected, however. She's not mingling in the ballroom. She's not helping elderly guests pick food from the buffet. She's not even soothing a five-year-old heiress who's crying because the pony took a shit.

I move through the throngs of people, smiling vaguely when people call me, returning a distracted handshake before plowing on. Where the hell is she? If they have her working in the goddamn kitchens again like a goddamn house elf, I'm going to lose it.

I'm passing through the large hallway leading to the art gallery when I see it—two members of the waitstaff gathering up broken glass from marble floors.

"What happened here?" I ask, leaning against the doorframe.

One of them widens her eyes. Nervous around a guest, maybe. Or nervous because of what just happened. There's a sense of panic in the air, more than comes from a broken crystal glass. "N-nothing, sir. Only cleaning up a small mess. I was clumsy."

"I don't think you were clumsy," I say, and she flinches even though my voice is soft. "But someone was. Where is he? Or she, I suppose? It could be either gender. Or neither of them, but somehow it's always a man causing problems, isn't it?"

She makes a small sound of denial, unwilling to share information. Except a quick dart of her eyes gives him away. Or her. I'll find out soon enough. I stride across the gallery floor, the heels of my Ferragamo Angiolos tapping on the stone. A heavy wooden door with ornate scrollwork guards one of the many antechambers. Salons, you could call them. Drawing rooms. Old world places for gathering in small groups. Or motel rooms, as they're more often called among the cousins, because they're always available for a quick fuck. No one bothers you here.

I knock on the door, expecting to find a belligerent guest vomiting on the Aubusson. Or a rowdy couple baptising the leather armchair.

The sight that greets me makes my blood run cold.

Bryant fucking Morelli, the patriarch of this family, the ex-CEO of Morelli Holdings, the host of this little shindig, stands there, face red, cursing profusely.

With his hand around Eva's wrist.

The skin around his grip has turned white from the pressure. There's fear in her wide eyes. And pain written in the tight line of her lips. He's hurting her.

And I see red.

CHAPTER THREE

Eva Morelli

D AMAGE CONTROL. THAT'S the only thing on my mind since my mother sent me from the ballroom. *Your father.* That was all she said. All she needed to say.

There was an emergency with the fake snow turning to ice. A horse-drawn carriage almost went down. And there was a disaster where someone had brought their purse dog and then let him loose.

Then my mother whispers those words, urgent, pained, and I know *this* is the emergency now.

I search the ballroom. The dining tables. Outside.

A group of people are drunkenly singing the refrain to *Hallelujah.*

The discordant notes send shivers down my spine.

I find my father in an antechamber off the art

gallery smashing glasses of champagne against the painting of our family as if they were baseballs in a batting cage.

Waitstaff hover outside the room, unable to stop him. Just as well that they don't get in his way. We don't need another ambulance called to the house.

Waitstaff get ambulances. Guests get ambulances.

Family? We get a first aid kit in an upstairs bathroom. We're used to Bryant Morelli's rampages, used to the shouting and the shoving and the bruises that inevitably follow.

I'm used to it. At least, that's what I tell myself as my father shakes me in anger, as he grasps my wrist. As I flinch away from his slap. He doesn't hurt me often, not anymore, but it still happens sometimes. The old desperation takes hold of me. Along with the fear.

Then the door swings open.

We freeze, my father in fury, me in shock.

Any number of people could have wandered back here. Everyone knows about the antechambers. The cleaning staff regularly has to pick up used condoms from the ten-thousand-dollar rugs after these galas. If it's a guest, they'll probably sense we're in a conflict and find another room.

They might gossip, but at least they'll go away.

It's not a random guest that stands there.

It's Finn Hughes. My heart thuds against my ribs. I barely have time to register him standing there, austere in his bespoke tux, his usually affable expression made dark.

Then he crosses the room in hard, floor-eating strides. He does something too fast for me to see, a blur, and then my hand is released. My father recoils with a grunt of pain. He pulls back, holding his arm against his side, snarling with indignation.

Then I can't see him anymore, because Finn steps between us.

My father is not a small man. He's solid. Strong for a man in his sixties. Terrifying when he's in a rage. The idea of Finn—charming, elegant Finn—being hit by his fists makes me cry out.

Except he doesn't get the chance.

Finn throws a punch, knocking my father back. Another punch. "You want to pick on someone? Pick on me. You want to fight? Fight someone who will fight back."

I've always known Finn was tall and lean. I never realized how strong he was. Not until he pushes my father against the wall and shoves him a foot off the ground—all two hundred and fifty pounds of him. He holds him up with one hand.

My father curses in gasping breaths.

Finn scoffs. "Oh, you're going to fuck me up? You and who else? Would your own sons back you up in a fight? Your brothers? You sure as hell can't take me yourself."

"I'll ruin you," my father rasps.

"You can't touch me, old man."

Adrenaline rushes through my veins. I run to grab his free arm. "Finn," I say, out of breath, panicky. "Please. Stop. You have to let him go."

Finn looks at me, hazel eyes made brilliant by violence. "Why? Because he'll punish you for this? I should break his fucking neck."

"No," I say, tears stinging my eyes, humiliation a hard knot in my stomach.

Some people might wonder why I want him spared, this man who runs rampant in my nightmares. He's hurt me in countless ways, but he's still my father. Flesh and blood. Family loyalty was drilled into me, etched into my skin, from the moment I was born. Love is tangled up in guilt and shame and duty. I can't even tell them apart.

None of this should make sense, but as Finn looks at me through those green and golden eyes,

I have the feeling he understands. "Fuck," he mutters, releasing my father in a single, quick move, letting him slump to the ground.

I take a step forward to stop him and then halt. Approaching him now would be like approaching a hungry crocodile—I could have my neck snapped in an instant.

"How dare you," my father says, glaring at Finn. "I'll have you run out of town. I'll have you horse whipped. I'll have you drowned in the fucking river."

Anyone would be scared when being threatened by him. He's powerful and wealthy—and vindictive. But Finn doesn't even seem concerned. He seems... contemptuous. As if he's watching a hornet wage war on a mountain. My blood pounds with anxiety. *Danger, danger, danger.* This is a terrible situation, but still, there's something so brave about Finn's nonchalance.

I wish I had his courage.

"You do that," Finn says, his voice colder than I've ever imagined it. This isn't a carefree playboy. This is a man with power and responsibilities. "Later. For now you're going to walk off that black eye. Anyone asks? You ran into a fucking door."

It seems impossible. Every part of me revolts

from the possibility, but somehow, the command works. My father swears the whole way out the door, muttering threats and curses, but he slinks away, out of the antechamber, leaving the door ajar behind him.

"Christ," Finn says, shutting the door.

"I'm sorry that happened," I say, babbling, shaking with nerves. "Please don't think—I mean, you must wonder how—I'm sure he didn't know—"

"He didn't know I would interrupt?" he asks, his voice dry. "I'm sure he didn't. Does that happen often? Him hurting you."

"He didn't hurt me." The lie comes out automatically.

He doesn't break eye contact as he crosses the plush rug. As he takes my arm, gentle even as he proves me wrong. His thumb brushes my wrist, and I wince. It's still red, the flesh burning where my father twisted it. I know from experience that it'll be blue tomorrow morning.

"Liar," he says, the accusation soft.

There's a hitch in my breath. "It's not that bad."

"It's worse. I knew he was an asshole, but I didn't know—Fuck, maybe I did know. Maybe the whole goddamn world knows how bad men can be, and we just let them do it."

"Don't," I say, a knot in my throat. Seeing him angry on my behalf... it does something to me. Makes me yearn and hope. Dangerous feelings. "Leo protected me."

A glance down at his wrist. "Where is he?"

It's not a real question. His tone says it's a challenge, like he's calling me a liar again. And maybe I am lying. Leo protected me. He got between me and my father countless times, taking beatings for me, fighting back—though he could never manage Finn's icy composure. We were all too heated for that. But he couldn't be around me twenty-four seven. He couldn't be there when he was at work. Or when he moved out. He couldn't be everywhere at once.

"You aren't going to tell anyone about this, are you?" I can only imagine my mother's horror at finding out that Finn Hughes saw my father in that state.

He shakes his head. "I should have killed him while I had the chance."

"No," I say, somehow managing a dry tone. "Then my mother would really freak out."

"She might thank me."

I run my hands along my arms, trying to control my shivers. It's the adrenaline. I recognize this feeling from other times my father rampaged through the house. My mother would retreat into her sitting room with a bottle of wine. My sisters would be jumpy and anxious. My brothers would often get into a fight even though the danger had passed. I've never felt that before, brimming over with violence, but somehow I'm feeling it now. Like I want to push Finn. Like I want to push him and pull him, but I wouldn't hurt him. No. I'd kiss him.

I shake my head, forcing the crazy thought away. "She would probably help you hide the body. You'd give her that insouciant smile, and she'd say, 'anything for a Hughes.'"

"Insouciant," he says, using that exact smile. Charming. Irreverent.

It shouldn't be possible, but he makes me smile, too. "That's what you are."

His warm hazel eyes take in the way I'm shaking, and he reaches out. He tucks me against his chest. For a moment, I hold myself rigid. I've been hugged a hundred times at the gala so far. Family, friends, acquaintances. Even strangers will hug me, drunk on my family's wine. Or because they want to get closer to my family's power. None of those hugs felt like this.

On a soft exhale, I let myself sink into his

arms.

He murmurs against my hair. "Who the hell uses words like insouciant? Except for The New Yorker."

"Lots of people use that word."

"What does it even mean?"

Strong. That's the first word that comes to mind, because I'm in his arms. I can feel the surprising hardness of his body beneath the smooth lines of the tux. *Strong and brave in the face of violence.* "It means nonchalant."

His lips move into a smile against my hair. "Another big word. Do you talk like that all the time?"

I make a small sound, more of a dismissal than an answer.

"You're different," he says. "Why are you different?" It doesn't come out like a question. It feels more like he's wondering something aloud, something he's thought before.

"I'm not different," I say, because I don't want him to get the wrong idea. I know why he's interested in me. Because I'm one of the only women he hasn't been with at the gala. I'm a novelty. Something new, but not special.

His fingers go beneath my chin. He tips my face up. Those hazel eyes look different this close.

A deeper green. The golden flecks shimmering. He's beautiful but opaque. It's impossible to see what he's really thinking or feeling. I have the sense that all his charm is a front. I don't know what lies beneath the playboy surface. Maybe no one does.

"Why did you come here?" I whisper.

A liason, most likely. A plan to meet up with one of the women at the gala. So why haven't they come? "I was looking for you," he murmurs.

"Why?" It feels like opening Pandora's box.

"To do this." That's all he says before he leans down. His mouth is an inch away from mine. He hovers there, letting his breath warm my lips, breathing me in.

He brushes against me. It's a tease, that faint touch. My nerve endings come alight. He kisses the way he talks—playful, laid back. I relax into his embrace. He licks the seam of my lips, and my breath catches. I push up on my toes, surging closer.

Easy, I think. It's easy to be with him. Maybe that's what *safe* feels like.

He nips my bottom lip, and I whimper.

A shiver captures me, head to toe. He pulls back. His eyes are deeper now, forest green, a place of mystery and magic.

This isn't insouciance. Or nonchalance.

It's something darker.

He tightens a fist in my hair, turning me around so I face the wall, holding me against his hard chest. It took so long to do my hair for tonight. Hours of shampoo and conditioner and blow drying. Making the curls just right. They're nothing but a handle for him now. Something stark and blatantly sexual.

I feel submissive this way. Trapped. My sex clenches beneath my evening gown.

"What are you doing?" I ask, breathless.

"Tasting," he murmurs, dragging kisses along my neck, biting the juncture to my shoulder. "I just want a taste. I won't hurt you. You aren't scared, are you?"

I'm alone in a room with a man—a strong, virile man. One who isn't afraid to shove someone against a wall. He's holding me in such a way that I can't defend myself. "Yes," I whisper.

An unsteady laugh. "That shouldn't turn me on so much."

A large hand passes over my breasts, as if he's an explorer, a marauder, mapping the terrain that he plans to claim as his own. He reaches beneath the neckline, and I gasp as his fingers rub across my nipples. I strain—whether to lean into his touch or get away, I don't know. It only manages to wind my hair tighter in his grasp. The sharp pull brings tears to my eyes.

"So that's what you've been hiding," he says, pinching my nipple until I gasp. "Acting demure and innocent when you have these beautiful breasts aching for attention."

As soon as he says the word I know it's true. They are aching, but he pulls his hand away. In between a single breath and the next he releases my hair and turns me back around to face him. We stand there, connected only by pain, by wanting. I've been to mass a million times, but this feels somehow more religious than every moment I've spent kneeling.

I want to kneel in front of this man. Want to worship him with my body.

He pulls me against his body, tight and secure, but I can't stop shivering. It's a different kind of shock than the one that comes after violence.

This is the echo of intimacy.

"More," I whisper.

"I'm not going to fuck you in a motel room," he says, his voice raw.

I breathe out a laugh. I've heard the antechambers called motel rooms before. Most of the cousins call them that, but I've never done anything here. Never even made out with a boy on these leather chairs. At this moment it seems like a massive oversight.

I've been too busy helping my mother.

Too busy being hurt by my father.

Footsteps sound outside the antechamber. Finn moves me behind him just as the door swings open. I peer around his arm to see my brother storm in, looking furious.

"Leo," I say on a gasp.

"So glad you could join us," Finn says, his tone unconcerned. "A family affair. Will all the Morellis be joining us? Not sure there's enough seating for everyone."

He's always ready for a joke, even when my father was here. Except this is worse. Bryant Morelli is wild, uncontrolled violence. My brother is a sharp blade.

He doesn't pause. He heads straight for us, straight for Finn, murder in his dark eyes. "Take your hands off my sister. I fucking warned you."

I'm stunned. "You *warned* him away from me? Why?"

"Because of this," Leo says, biting out the words. "Because he's putting his fucking hands on you, another Constantine. He's *using* you."

"Another Constantine?" Finn says, catching onto that detail immediately.

There's a dark secret in my past, something Finn can never find out about. No one can find out about it. It would humiliate me, but that's not the only reason. It's a loose thread in the black fabric of our family history. If someone were to pull, the whole thing could unravel.

Chapter Four

Finn Hughes

"DON'T FUCKING TALK to her," Leo says, advancing.

He wants to fight me. And part of me wants to fight him. It's perverse, but I'm angry at him for not protecting Eva better. Maybe what I wanted from him is superhuman. He couldn't really have shadowed her every second of the night. But I hate that I found her at the mercy of her asshole father. I want someone to pay for that. Him. Me. Maybe both of us deserve to be pummeled for that ring of red around her wrist.

"What are you going to do?" I taunt him, pushing Eva back, because she's struggling to get between us. She doesn't want me hurting her hot-tempered brother. Or maybe it's me she doesn't want hurt. "Kill every man at the gala? They all want her, you know."

"I'll start with you." Dark eyes flash. "Then see how I feel."

"No, don't," Eva says, pushing in front of me, defending me with her small body. It's enough to make her brother stop, at least. Which is a good thing. If he'd put his hands on her, if he'd pushed her aside or hurt her in any way, I would have lost my shit. "Don't," she says again, and whatever he sees in her expression makes him curse softly.

She turns to me, her dark eyes pleading. God, those eyes. So full of sorrow and mystery. They make me want to slay every dragon, starting with the overbearing brother. "Just go."

"He doesn't get to tell you who to talk to," I say, pissed on her behalf.

"Please," she begs. It's my undoing.

"Christ."

She stands there looking vulnerable and strong, delicate and defiant. I want to consume her. I want to save her. In the end I can do nothing. Her brother doesn't get to order her around. I don't either. If she wants me to leave, then I will.

It's a test of willpower to leave her there. I push past her brother, bumping his shoulder the way he bumped mine earlier, making it clear this isn't over.

I'm leaving because she asked me to—not because of him.

There's a surreal quality to the gala when I return to the ballroom. The music. The whirl of dancers. The ornate gold swags hanging on the walls. All of it feels like a luxury funhouse mirror, everything distorted and different. All because I held Eva in my arms. Because I tasted her. She trembled for me. I still feel the slight vibration of her against my skin, the warmth of her against my palms. I form a fist, as if I can keep the sensation inside.

I watch Sarah Morelli hold court, a queen in this particular castle. She's too austere to be a social butterfly, but it works in this setting— noble and superior, like a queen in her court. People fawn over her elaborate dress, the beautiful decorations. Waiters emerge from the kitchens with trays of mince pies—the pies that Eva worked on.

I'm standing in the ballroom, but I feel a million miles away from these people. I'm still back in that antechamber. Still wrapped around Eva's sweet, panting body.

Daphne Morelli, Eva's younger sister, hovers on the other side. She stands with a young blonde I recognize as Haley Constantine, the woman Leo's with. From the corner of my eye I see Lucian and his lady-love make a quick exit.

I've been to a million events like this, but suddenly I feel out of place. It's not the gala that changes. It's me. As if the touch of Eva's lips shifted some small, crucial part of me.

Great.

I stride through the other side of the ballroom, passing a couple making out beneath a heavy garland of mistletoe. It's darker back here. This leads away from the public wing, into the family spaces. I've been here before during intimate dinner parties.

Never upstairs, though.

I climb the wide, sweeping staircase. Deep carpet hides my footsteps.

A worried servant steps out of a door at the end of the hall, holding a first aid kit. Bingo.

"Is he inside?" I ask when he approaches, my voice pleasant.

The man looks nervous. "No one's supposed to be up here."

I pull out a few hundreds from my billfold. "I'm a close friend of the family."

That's enough to make him hurry away. No loyalty. It doesn't speak well of how the family treats their employees. But it serves my purpose right now. I enter the room.

"I told you to leave me the fuck alone." The

words are slurred. He was already drunk downstairs. And I'm guessing he's been drinking steadily since he left.

"You don't sign my paycheck," I say, crossing the dark library. I stop at the ice-coated window, looking down at the revelry on the lawn, where a snowball fight has broken out.

Worry. Anger. Resentment. Through the window's reflection I watch those emotions play over Bryant Morelli's battered face. He wants to demand that I leave. More than that, he wants to take his rage out on me, but he must know I'd love any excuse to punch him again.

"What the hell are you doing here?" he finally asks, sounding resigned.

"Having a conversation."

"About what?"

I watch as one of the Morelli cousins, Charles, packs a snowball down hard.

He aims. Fires. It lands in the face of Maise Dunlevy.

That's got to hurt. I can hear her shrieking from the second story, through thick glass. It's like watching a live action snowglobe. She was Miss New Jersey Teen a couple years back. Now she's hunting for a rich husband to refill her parent's coffers.

Pageant coaches don't come cheap.

"About *what*?" Morelli demands again.

"About how you're not going to lay a finger on your daughter."

"I don't care what she told you. She's always been a willful, spoiled child."

"And you've always been a terrible liar. Why the hell Sarah Morelli stays with you, I have no idea. But I don't think she'd stand by you if you lost the money. Or the power."

"How dare you," he sputters. "You're nothing. A fucking *child*."

I don't bother looking at him when we talk. He'll notice the slight. I'm twenty-nine years old. Young, compared to Bryant Morelli. Young compared to others in the game of money and power. It doesn't stop me. "Is that so? You haven't heard any rumors? You haven't heard whispers? Then you're even less well-connected than I thought."

In the reflection, his eyes widen. Those same dark eyes that Eva has. It's unnerving, the similarity. That's the irony of family, I suppose. He's heard the rumors. That's the important thing.

Eva has her secrets. I haven't forgotten what Leo said. *Another Constantine?* Who was the first?

Well, I'll find out. She isn't the only one with secrets, though.

Hers are probably innocent. Mine are god-damn gruesome, but it doesn't matter. At the moment it's something I'm using to my advantage.

"Do we have an understanding?" I ask.

Silence. Then, "Yes."

Without a word I leave the room and retrace my steps down the carpeted staircase. The gala has lost its appeal. I text my driver to pick me up at the entrance. It's time to go.

Bryant Morelli will keep his promise, for now. Because he's afraid of me. He should be, but eventually he'll forget. Eventually he'll hurt her again. She's too loyal to walk away from her family, no matter how toxic and abusive they are.

I'll have to watch over her from a distance.

I can't have Eva Morelli, but I can protect her from afar.

Thank you for reading this story set in the lush and seductive Midnight Dynasty world! Eva and Finn meet again... You can read the angsty + swoony story now...

Finn Hughes knows about secrets. His family is as wealthy as the Rockefellers. And as powerful as the Kennedys. He runs the billion-dollar corporation. No one knows that he has a ticking time clock on his ability to lead.

Eva Morelli is the oldest daughter. The responsible one. The caring one. The one who doesn't have time for her own interests.

Especially not her interest in the charismatic, mysterious Finn Hughes.

A fake relationship is the answer to both their problems.

Want to read more? Turn the page to read the first three chapters of ONE FOR THE MONEY right now...

Extended Excerpt from One for the Money

Chapter One

Eva

BLACK TUXEDOS. GLITTERING gowns. Splashing champagne.

These things are common in my life. Mundane. I grew up under the warm glow of chandeliers. Laughter and conversation were my lullabies, the sound drifting up the spiral staircase to our bedrooms. I learned the planning of these events from my mother, the same way other daughters learn to quilt or bake or garden.

This particular gala benefits the Society for the Preservation of Orchids.

Ironic, considering the number of orchids we had to kill to build the elaborate sculpture in the foyer. My mother sits on the board. She doesn't care about flowers.

She cares about connections.

It's the family business, really. Making deals in ballrooms.

My father waves me over to him. He's officially retired. Stepped down as CEO of Morelli Holdings. Replaced by my brother Lucian. Unofficially, he'll only stop working when he's six feet underground. It's just the way he was made.

"Hi, Dad." I give him a dutiful kiss on his cheek.

He pulls me close to his side. His mood is magnanimous. Probably because there's a congressman, a famous filmmaker, and an oil tycoon from Texas hanging on his every word. "This is my daughter, Eva. Have you met her? She's the one responsible for all this."

The group responds with enthusiastic praise.

"The arbor is absolutely inspired," the filmmaker says. "The way you used crepe paper to mimic the tree bark, the way the branches wind above you. It feels like you're walking through a real forest. If you ever want to do set design, you have a place in L.A."

My father's hand tightens on my arm. "We could never let her go."

I manage a gracious smile. "High praise, indeed. But you're right. I could never leave New

York. It's home."

The oil tycoon winks. "That's right. I tried to lure her down to Texas. Unlimited barbecue and a swimming pool as big as a basketball court couldn't sway her."

My cheeks flush with old embarrassment. The man is handsome enough, in a white-haired kind of way. Smart enough. And definitely rich enough. But he didn't even bother asking me out. No, he went straight to my father and offered to buy me in a business deal.

As if I were a head of cattle.

I excuse myself and stride away, directing a server to refill their glasses. I know what each of them likes to drink. I know where their vacation homes are and what racehorses they own. It's part of my role as hostess, to make everyone comfortable.

To make everyone comfortable except for me.

My face feels tight from smiling. My feet ache from running around all day. I wore flats until the gala started, then I switched into heels, but it didn't help. My calves are burning.

Since things are smooth in the ballroom, I swing through the kitchen. One of the cooks is shouting obscenities at a server who dropped a plate of appetizers. Even I have to cringe at the loss. Each large white spoon contains a thin slice of Japanese Shorthorn Wagyu beef with caviar and mascarpone cream, topped with delicately sliced jalepeños, red onion, and Asian pear.

"Clean this up," I say to the server, mostly to get him away from the cook. Will he hire him again? Maybe not, but there's no point making him cry in the middle of service. Then I address the cook. "Do we have any more of that caviar?"

"Yes," he growls, still frustrated. "None of the beef."

"Serve it on crostini with crème fraîche."

"I don't serve boring food."

"You do unless you want the people to go home hungry."

He curses fluently but turns to prepare the tray. My work here is done. For now, anyway. I head back upstairs. On the way I pass the head bartender, who looks harried.

"We're out of champagne," he says, panic in his voice.

"How is that possible?"

The top of his bald head shines with sweat. He used to be a top sommelier at a five-star hotel, but a few hundred of Bishop's Landing's elite reduces him to a nervous breakdown. "Some young men. They wanted the bottles for beer pong. Champagne pong, they called it."

"And you gave it to them?"

"Of course not." He looks indignant. Then he sighs. "Mrs. Crockett asked after that vintage of Chardonnay she likes, and I went down to the wine cellar to get it. Then when I got back, two entire cases of champagne were gone."

I press two fingers to the middle of my forehead. No champagne. If we aren't careful, we'll have a full-scale revolt on our hands. "We have white wine, right?"

"Plenty, madam."

"The signature cocktail of the night is now a white wine spritzer, designed to celebrate both the simplicity and the depth of orchids. Have the bartenders offer it first. If we're giving them something delicious and sparkling, they should be content."

"And if someone requests champagne specifically?"

"There's a couple bottles of Armand de Brignac in my father's study." Which I'll have to replace before he notices it's gone. He won't appreciate having his private stash picked over. Then again, he wouldn't like to have the guests denied.

That crisis averted, I continue working my

way through the room.

My mother waves me over. "There's someone I want you to meet," she says, and she's already smiling. Which means he must be nearby. And powerful.

"Who?" I know the entire guest list for this event, which means I know everyone in the room. Maybe not personally, but I know their names and their net worth. Those are the main things that matter in high-society circles.

An older man waits near the balcony door. He wears the black tuxedo well. He clearly works out. And if his hairline is receding, well, he can hardly help that. He looks to be in his forties, maybe ten years older than me. I recognize him as being in the manufacturing industry. "You must be Mr. Langley," I say.

"I see my reputation precedes me," he says, laughing. "Call me Alex."

"How long are you staying in New York?" I ask, being polite. He's got factories throughout the flyover states, but his home is in Chicago if I remember correctly.

"For a long time, perhaps. I'm thinking of moving to the East Coast."

"Are you?" I say, my stomach sinking as I realize why my mother wanted to introduce us.

It's her attempt at matchmaking. The irony is that if I actually got married and started my own family, my mother would probably have a nervous breakdown. My father would get arrested for being drunk and disorderly. And my siblings would need something from me. Having money smooths a lot of life's hard edges, but it doesn't blunt them completely. We still need someone to handle the details. To get my mother her Xanax, to call the lawyer. To de-escalate every situation. We need a manager. And in the Morelli family, ever since I turned fifteen, that's me.

He gives me a vaguely paternal smile. "It's time for me to start a family."

Not exactly subtle, Alex. "I wish you luck, then."

"Eva planned this little gala," my mother says, breezing past my comment. "She creates the most memorable displays. People talk about them for months."

"The perfect hostess," he says, clearly approving.

Bile rises in my throat. Now I know what a racehorse feels like when it's being checked over. *Good teeth. A friendly disposition. Will look nice pulling your carriage.*

"Speaking of hosting, I should check back in

the kitchens."

I make a break for it, but my mother catches up with me. She leads me into an empty hallway and a darkened drawing room.

"Sit with me," she says. "I feel like we've been circling all night. I haven't had a chance to really see you."

"I'm right here."

We *have* been circling all night. That's what we always do, me managing one side of the room while she manages the other. We even do it at family dinners, her with my father, me handling my brothers. We spend untold energy keeping the peace in the Morelli household.

She hands me a glass filled with spritzer.

"It's very good," she says.

She usually doesn't leave this long in the middle of a gala. "Can I get you anything?"

"Langley is worth a nice seven billion."

"Mother."

She adopts an innocent expression. "Do you *want* to marry someone poor?"

"I don't want to marry anyone. And definitely not Alex Langley."

"His wife died five years ago. He's been mourning her. Sweet, don't you think?"

"Then why are you trying to set us up?"

"If you must know, he asked after you. He's ready to start a family. He wants someone mature, closer in age to him than the debutantes, but still beautiful. You fit the bill."

"How flattering."

All of us wear masks. My mother is the exquisite beauty and perfect hostess. She lets the mask slip only rarely. I've only met the true Sarah Morelli a handful of times.

This is one of those times.

Her green eyes are an endless field. "Not flattering, Eva. No. Don't look to men for flattery. Not if you want to be someone's wife. Flattery is for their girlfriends. Their mistresses. Their whores. Not the women by their sides."

"Why would I want to be someone's wife?"

"Security. Connections. Children. The same reasons women have gotten married for hundreds of years. Thousands of years, probably. Humans haven't evolved that far."

"Then it won't matter much if the evolutionary line ends with me."

The wall goes back up. In the blink of an eye I'm looking at the serene expression of a society hostess, as remote and poised as anyone. Not my mother. "You'll want children eventually. All women do. Don't wait too long."

I've heard that line before. There are arguments I could make. *Not all women want to be mothers. And that's fine. Feminism is about letting women choose their own path.*

The words stick in my throat.

Not all women want to be mothers, but in my secret heart, I do.

"Is now really the time?" I ask, my words tight.

"You have to settle down at some point."

"Why?"

"So you have your own home."

"I'm not homeless, Mom."

"A real home, not a loft filled with knick-knacks. A husband can give you that."

"This is the twenty-first century. And in case you haven't noticed, I'm loaded. I could buy a house if I wanted. I already own houses, actually."

"Places," she says. "Buildings. Not homes."

"Because it doesn't have a penis in it?"

Her eyelids flutter closed. "Eva Honorata Morelli."

I look past her toward the large picture window. "The truth is that I would like children, but I'm not willing to live in a loveless marriage for that."

It's beautiful out there. Green and maintained

and lush. Beautiful the way the inside of the house is beautiful. Grand and a little intimidating. It's the kind of house I would preside over if I made a society marriage to someone like Langley.

Her tone is conciliatory. "There's security for a woman in marriage."

"And give up my freedom?"

"My relationship with your father is complicated. It doesn't have to be that way for you. The man I just introduced you to is a good man. You can trust him."

"I can't trust anyone," I say flatly. Because I can't. Security? Acceptance in society? That's not what you get when you go with a man. That's not what you bet on. Ever.

My mother studies me, looking bemused. We're close as far as mothers and daughters go, but I've never told her why I don't trust men. And I won't be telling her tonight.

The door to the sitting room opens.

A man stands there in a tux that speaks of wealth and a bearing that says his family has had it for generations. Privilege. Power. And enough self-awareness to make it feel like an inside joke that you're part of. Phineas Hughes was a few years behind me when I came up in society. We've met. And everyone knows about them. The

Hughes family is like the Kennedys or the Vanderbilts—steeped in luxury. Though we've never spoken for very long.

Blonde hair gleams beneath the low lighting.

Hazel eyes twinkle with roguish charm.

"Finn Hughes," my mother exclaims, her cheeks pinkening, her eyes going bright.

She lifts her glass just a little, and I wish I had a Diet Coke instead of the spritzer. I feel my own cheeks heating, but I don't flutter my eyelashes like my mother does. I don't act surprised to see him, even though I have no idea what he's doing here.

"Mrs. Morelli," Finn says with a playful bow. He doesn't need to be handsome or well-built. Not when he's the oldest son of one of the most powerful families in the country. He's painfully rich, but that doesn't stop him from also being charming. It's honestly annoying.

"I told you to call me Sarah," my mother scolds, flirting with a man half her age.

"Mrs. Morelli," he says, refusing her with so much grace and respect that she can't be offended. "It's always a pleasure to see you again. I came looking for your daughter."

Excitement rushes through me like champagne, like caffeine. Me?

"Sophia's not here," my mother says.

She assumes a playboy like Finn Hughes, a man who could have whoever he wants, would want Sophia. She's the wild child. The one who could have adventures with him. And suddenly I feel old at the ripe old age of thirty-three. I don't go to exclusive night clubs. I don't get into trouble, if I can help it.

Instead I help my mother plan her events and help my siblings manage their lives. I help and help and help, and it never seemed quite so depressing until this moment.

My stomach sinks.

"I want Eva," he says, glancing at me. That devilish glint in his eyes promises mischief. And maybe even danger. It promises something entirely different than *help*. "We have plans."

He's lying, of course.

Though I don't know why.

Maybe he just wants to save me from this awkward conversation. Or maybe he really does need help—perhaps the lack of champagne has finally created chaos.

Sophia would be right for Finn. That's assuming he's ever looking to settle down, which I doubt. Wealthy. Handsome. And far too charming. Why would such a man choose marriage? My mother was right about one thing. Marriage does have more benefits for the woman.

Men can do whatever they want.

Women like me? We have a ticking clock. There's only so long that I'll stay attractive to men like Langley. Only so long that I can have children. My heart squeezes thinking of all the years I've spent being helpful. Thinking of all the years I've spent trying to make sure that my family had what they needed. Paying attention to everything and everyone. Except myself.

And now it might be too late.

CHAPTER TWO

Finn

WE DON'T HAVE plans.

I made that up three minutes ago when I walked by and heard Sarah Morelli trying to set up her daughter with that older man from the gathering. I couldn't leave her there alone.

Alex fucking Langley for Eva? He's ancient.

Maybe not that much older than her, not so much older that it would be a scandal, but he's old. And boring. He's searching for a mate the way you find a mare for a stallion. For well-bred children. That's what these men want, a woman to bring them a drink at the end of the day, to be the hostess at events like this one. Plan everything, so he never has to think about anything. Do everything, so he only has to glad-hand at galas.

I'm going to get her out of here.

Surprise flashes through Sarah Morelli's eyes.

I know what I look like to her. A catch. She's put me next to Lizzy at past dinner parties, as if I might be interested in a child. We might be in the twenty-first century, but matches are still made. Arranged marriages happen every day in families like ours.

No, thank you.

I won't be getting married. Ever.

And I'm not particularly interested in the Morellis. Except for Eva. There's something about her that calls to me. The sense of innate sadness. It makes me want to cheer her up, which is something I can do—at least in a temporary way.

That's what I'm good for. Temporary.

"You didn't tell me you had plans," Sarah tells Eva, half scolding. The delighted smile on her face gives her away. It may surprise her, but she's nothing if not adaptable. Bagging a Hughes with any daughter would be a coup. "Where are you going?"

"Yes, Finn. Where are we going?" Eva asks, laughter in her voice.

I like this mischievous Eva better than the beleaguered one. Her dark eyes sparkle with silent challenge. It makes me hard beneath the thin wool of my tux. "It's a surprise."

"Indeed," Sarah murmurs, glancing between the two of us.

Suspicious? Perhaps, but she's not going to say

no to me. Not because I'm persuasive or charming. She won't say no because my family is one of the most wealthy and powerful in the country. I could be a bastard, and Sarah would still hand me her daughter on a silver platter.

Eva's wine-red lips quirk in a half-smile. "As much fun as surprises can be, I think I should stay here. After the champagne drought, who knows what might go wrong?"

"We ran out of champagne?" Sarah glances at her almost-empty champagne glass. "Is that why we have a white wine spritzer as the signature cocktail? It's delicious, but I don't remember seeing it in the event plan."

It's time to issue my own subtle challenge to Eva Morelli. Enough of the event planning and the matchmaking. I'm strangled for air, and I've only been here a few minutes.

It's like she's being buried alive with piles of money.

"I can't tell you where we're going," I admit. "But I can tell you what we'll be doing. We're going to have a good time. Fun. You remember how to do that, don't you?"

A delicate snort.

"So much fun you'll lose track of time."

"Promises, promises."

"I don't make promises I don't keep," I tell her, looking into her dark, fathomless eyes. There's not much I can offer this woman, but I can offer her this.

Eva's expression flickers with wariness. And with curiosity.

Her mother looks scandalized by Eva's reaction to me. In another second, she'll open her mouth and demand that her daughter come with me. But I don't want Eva to come because her mother demands it. I want her to come because she chooses curiosity.

No, I want her to come because she chooses me.

I lean against the doorframe as if I have all the time in the world. Really, the opposite is true. "How about a bet? If you have a good time tonight, then I win. But if you, in your honest assessment, don't have a good time, you win."

"I'll win what, exactly?"

I reach into my pockets. A billfold. An old pocket watch. A handful of coins.

The quarter flips off my thumb and across the room. I didn't give her enough warning, but she captures it anyway. Delicate fingers smooth across the warm metal. "Twenty-five cents? I suppose I could add foam to my Starbucks order tomorrow."

"Have a wonderful meal," Sarah Morelli says.

Eva kisses her mother's cheek.

When she approaches me, her chin is high and her bearing regal, but there's a hint of vulnerability in her eyes. It's what pulls me to her. She's so damn strong, holding up her entire family like Atlas holds the world. But who rubs her shoulders at the end of the day?

I offer her my arm, and she takes it. Very formal.

There's nothing untoward about us. My body doesn't give a fuck. It reacts with a violent sense of victory. *Mine,* it says. The way her arm rests in mine, the heat of her body—it's like she was made to stand at my side.

Or maybe I was made to stand by hers.

Which is all just my body's way of telling me I'm down to fuck.

I don't think that's in the cards for me tonight, but I find I don't mind that much. The challenge is more appealing. The challenge to make Eva Morelli have fun. I escort her out of the room. We're all the way down the hall when she starts second-guessing herself. I feel it enter her limbs like stiffness. Like fear, even if she'd never admit it.

"We don't actually have to go anywhere," she murmurs, as if she's letting me off the hook. As if I should be relieved that I don't get to take her on a date.

"Chickening out already?" I ask.

Her glance is sharp. "Excuse me?"

"That's what this is, right? You're afraid I might actually make good on my promise. That you'd actually have a good time, while your family has to fend for themselves."

Rose blooms on her cheeks. A deep breath draws my attention to the shadowed space between her breasts. Indignation looks sexy on her. "Unlike my mother, I know that there weren't any real plans. You only said that to shock her. This is a game for you."

"A game?"

"A game," she says, "like everything else in your life. You have money and women and cars, and not a single problem that can't be solved by a check."

Anger blisters through my veins. Followed by grief. "If you say so."

"My mother's going to expect me to come up with fantastical tales of this surprise date I somehow managed to land with the charming and handsome Finn Hughes."

"You think I'm handsome?"

An exasperated laugh. "She thinks you're handsome. I think you're annoying."

"You think I'm charming, for sure."

"And full of yourself."

I grin. "Come on, Morelli. Have a good time. I double-dog dare you."

She throws up her hands in the middle of the large, darkened hallway. "I can't even imagine leaving in the middle of a gala. What if something goes wrong?"

"Let it burn. We've got plans."

She shakes her head, a half-smile on her face. It's not refusal. It's the look of a woman who's going to let me show her a good time. I take her hand and lead her away from the bright lights. We leave through a side exit. Gargoyles watch us from the crown of the house as we go down. My Bugatti is already waiting there. I texted the valet before I even entered the drawing room. She's already purring in the gravel drive.

"Your car is already waiting?" Eva says, a laugh in her voice.

"What? I don't do half-assed promises. I stole you away for the night. You're mine for the next five hours. What will I do with you? I have ideas, of course. Hundreds of them." I sweep open the door and hold it for her.

Eva hesitates for a heartbeat. Then she lets me hand her into the deep seat.

"Where are we really going?" she says. "Somewhere in the city?"

"No, somewhere here."

"Here as in Bishop's Landing?" she says. Because, of course, Eva grew up here.

She should know the places a person would go to have fun in Bishop's Landing. And I don't mean champagne fun, I mean alcohol fun. I mean blackout-and-forget fun. Or at least the possibility of it. The possibility of bliss.

"Yes," I tell her.

"Will you take me home afterward?"

"Back to your parents' house?" I ask.

"I don't live in the Morelli mansion," she says.

No, of course she doesn't. She lives in the city, but you wouldn't know it by how often she's here. Eva is always at her mother's society events.

She's always everywhere her family is.

"I'll take you home," I promise, knowing, even as I say it, that I'm never going to be able to drop her off at some ritzy loft in the city and drive away. I'll be thinking of her straight through the next year, and maybe even after that. I'll keep thinking and thinking and thinking until the thoughts turn into something filthy and rough, because I felt her body against mine.

It's a short drive to the small downtown of Bishop's Landing. I hook a right at an Italian restaurant that serves thin-crust pizzas as big as their tables. I keep driving down the alley. Cars gleam in a neat row behind closed businesses. Only one door has sound behind it.

During the day it's an art gallery. Right now it's something else entirely.

"Where are we?" she asks, whispering.

"The gallery. Don't you recognize it?"

"Are we going to steal a painting?"

"No, but I like the way you think. We can do that another night." I make a *tsk*ing sound when she tries to object. "But never fear. What we're about to do is also illegal."

Her eyes go wide in the dark. "*Finn.*"

I like her saying my name in that urgent, breathy way.

My body hardens. I'm having explicit ideas of ways I can take Eva in this alley. She'd probably like them, too. I've learned that high-society women enjoy a bit of roughness. They want something that silk sheets and bubble baths can't give them.

I knock on the door three times.

In the faint moonlight, Eva gazes up at me. She looks exhilarated, fully alive, and breathtakingly beautiful. It makes me want to corrupt her in every way I can imagine.

CHAPTER THREE

Eva

I'VE BEEN TO countless showings at this art gallery.

Apparently they deal in more than sculpture.

Clay pieces move across baize-covered tables. Alcohol flows freely. The underground poker club is in full swing when we arrive.

"How come I never knew about this place?"

"Overprotective brothers," Finn says with a shrug.

"Leo knows about this?" I ask, but then of course he does.

He knows everything that happens in Bishop's Landing and most things that happen in New York City. It would have been just like him to come here in his wild youth—and not tell me. His best friend. We're close, even for siblings.

But I can't quite shake the protectiveness out of him. "I'm going to kill him."

A fight breaks out over a table. Playing cards

fly. Men in suits break it up.

It's over in a flash, but I find myself behind Finn. Somehow, in those few seconds, he put himself between me and danger. A shiver runs through me. A delicious one. That fistfight was a reminder that this *is* illegal. But playboy or not, Finn Hughes will protect me.

For this night only, he's mine.

"You okay?" he murmurs, his gaze assessing me, seeing if I'm freaked out by the fight. *Chickening out already?* he asked before we left. I'm determined to prove him wrong.

I make a show of looking at a nonexistent watch. "I'm okay, but it looks like you're on your way to losing twenty-five cold, hard cents in that bet."

"You don't stand a chance, sweetheart."

He leads me down a narrow staircase into an even darker room, with fewer tables and a singer wearing a sparkling dress. The high roller room. Of course a Hughes would be allowed into any room, but it's interesting to me that they don't even ask.

They know him by sight.

Glasses clink. Chips clack. Low laughter rolls beneath it all.

Finn puts down a small stack of hundreds.

It's immediately replaced by chips.

He puts the entire stack in front of me.

I feel my eyes go wide. "This is too much."

"I know what you're worth, Morelli."

It's not that I'm a frugal person. I was raised in luxury, and I like nice things. Money doesn't impress me. That's what comes from being raised an heiress.

I wouldn't blink an eye at an expensive dinner or some other purchase.

"Listen, I understand trading money for things. But I don't understand gambling. It's trading money for... what? Risk? The chance to lose everything?"

"For fun, sweetheart. Don't you ever pay for fun?"

A snort is not quite a ladylike answer. But it's true. Even the money I spend on behalf of my family doesn't feel recreational. No, it's about society. Status. And business.

I run my fingertip along the stack of clay chips.

It's a lot of money to spend on fun. And maybe I don't feel like I deserve it.

The dealer calls for the ante, and I push forward five hundred-dollar markers. That's the entry amount. The minimum to play the game.

It makes my heart pound.

Or maybe it's Finn, standing so close to my stool.

He's only standing so close because the rest of the stools are full, I'm sure. He's only leaning near me so he can see the cards on the table. If my heart beats faster, that's only because it's been so long since I've had a man's warm breath brush my temple. Since I've felt a man against my back, almost intimate despite the public setting.

Cards are dealt.

I don't play at casinos, underground or otherwise, but I know the basics. The pairs and the straights and the flushes. Which is how I know the cards in my hand are a whole lot of nothing. Suddenly that five-hundred-dollar ante feels like a fortune. It feels like a loss.

Why did I think this would be a good idea?

Disappointment sinks in my gut.

Then a low voice murmurs in my ear. "Patience. Good things come to those who wait."

My breath catches at the masculine purr. It feels like sex surrounding me, sensual cashmere that makes my eyes close. "I've been waiting a long time."

I'm not sure where the words come from. I didn't feel like I was waiting. I'm not Aurora sleeping in a forest, dreaming of a kiss from Prince Charming.

I have no interest in kisses.

And Finn Hughes is no Prince Charming.

He puts his hand on my hip. His thumb brushes my skin through the silk of my dress, back and forth, back and forth. It's startling. Intimate. It could be excused as a casual gesture between friends. The natural result of close proximity. Almost.

Except that it's faintly possessive.

I don't feel like a possession to be bought and sold. I don't even feel like a head of cattle to be bargained for. No, I feel like a jewel. Something to be coveted.

Something to hold close so that no one else steals it.

He caresses me through the bids, through the flop and the turn cards. I'm left with a single pair of eights. Not exactly auspicious, but better than nothing.

The dealer waits for the round of bidding before the river.

This is the last card, the one that determines my hand for good.

So far none of the other players seem like they have incredible cards, but maybe they're hiding it well. Then again, two of the men seem enamored with the women who surround them. Three women for two men. And while the men wear suits, the women wear barely-there dresses that are more like glittering swimsuits. Not that I'm judging.

It just makes me feel old in my Dior ballgown.

It's not the ballgown. No, it's my actual age that makes me feel old.

Thirty-three is ancient for an unmarried woman in our social set.

We're waiting for the couple beside us to place their bet. They have to confer over every decision, using the opportunity to feel each other up.

They look deeply in love. Or deeply in lust. I'm not sure I even know the difference.

I glance back at the man who watches me.

His hazel eyes deepen to emerald as he looks back. "Go all in."

A startled laugh escapes me, but with our faces this close, my amusement dries up. It's replaced with whatever that couple has—not love, then. Lust. I feel my body become liquid and heavy, as if I'm readying myself. I'm in a room full of people, but my body doesn't care about that. It wants to take this man. "You're insane."

"I'm interesting," he counters, his lip curling up.

"You're reckless."

"I'm interested," he says, and I know what he means. His tone makes it clear. His gaze does, too. He's interested in me, the same way the man is interested in the woman he's practically fingering on the stool next to us.

The dealer clears his throat so that they'll make their bid.

"You're young," I tell him, because it's the reason we can't be together. Not the real reason, but one that's socially acceptable. I'm not some aging widow who has a fling with the pool boy. Men his age don't hook up with women my age.

"Bullshit," he says.

"How old are you?"

"Twenty-nine."

I scoff. "Young."

His smile turns a little sad. "Age isn't about how long you've lived."

"That's *exactly* what it's about."

"It's about experience." He leans close, so he can whisper. His lips brush the outer shell of my ear as he speaks, raising sparks of interest throughout my body. "And I think I have lots more experience than you. Don't worry, though. I'll break you in slowly."

"Break me *in*," I say, my voice too high. "Like I'm a horse."

"Don't be offended. My horses are thorough-breds."

I know from society talk that Hughes race-horses are legendary. But I didn't know how much of that legacy trickled down to Finn. Enough, apparently. "I'm not a thoroughbred."

"Ma'am," the dealer says, snagging my attention.

The couple made their decision. They're in.

It's my turn. Two pair probably isn't enough to win this. But I'm only one diamond away from a flush. On the off chance I get it, that could be enough to win.

Or it might not be.

I don't like the uncertainty. It makes me nervous. Anxious.

Or maybe that's the way Finn watches me. As if he wants to prove a point. That I'm staid, dependable Eva Morelli. That I wouldn't know how to have fun if it kidnapped me and took me to an underground casino.

I push the piles of chips into the center.

A gasp sounds from the people around the

table.

"Fuck," Finn murmurs, his hand tightening on my hip. "That was so hot."

The couple groans in unison and throws their cards down, quitting outside of their turn. The dealer brings the bet around again. Against my high raise, only one man remains. An elderly gentleman who looks severe with a poker face.

He looks, in Finn's words, experienced. I don't think he'd stay in with a poor hand.

Every muscle in my body clenches as I watch the dealer's hand.

He flips a card.

I blink, sure that I'm imagining it. An eight of diamonds sits on the green fabric. Holy shit. I got the flush that I was hoping for, but even more than that, I got a full house.

My fist shoots in the air. "*Yes.*"

Immediately my cheeks heat at the unladylike action.

Finn releases a low chuckle.

We're hardly being subtle, but it doesn't matter. There are already several thousand dollars in the pot. The older gentleman reveals a straight with a rueful smile.

"Congratulations," he tells me in a gruff voice.

Excitement overtakes my good sense and my

dignity. I throw my arms around Finn's neck, laughing. His eyes sparkle blue and green hues. "I told you good things would come to those who wait," he says, his voice low and private. They aren't suggestive words, not really. But I feel the erotic suggestion throughout my body, at the tips of my breasts and between my legs. As if he's rewarding me after a long, tantric session.

"I'm thirty-three," I tell him, waiting for his shock, his stiffness.

Dreading the way he'll have to force a smile.

He searches my eyes. "Do you think that matters to me?"

"You're a playboy. A rascal. You can have your pick of any woman inside this casino. And any woman outside of it. Why would you want me?"

"A rascal," he says, laughing. "Who says rascal anymore?"

Despite my embarrassment, despite my awkwardness, I find myself laughing with him. Laughing so hard tears prick my eyes. "See? I told you. I'm an old grandma."

He shakes with silent humor before becoming serious again. "Eva. You're an incredibly sexy woman. A bombshell. A goddamn dream. Any man would want you, me included."

I stop breathing for a ten count. "You do?"

"Men must make passes at you all the time. Women, too."

A knot forms in my throat.

"But you don't believe them," he guesses. "You think they're after your money."

I force a shrug. "It's not unlikely. You know what I'm worth. So do other people. They want my money or even just my connections to my family. But that's not why I don't pay attention when someone makes a pass at me."

"Then why?"

"Because I'm over love." The words come out fast and honest. It scares me, how much I liked the excitement. Winning. How much I wanted to do it again. How much I enjoy having Finn's thumb brush my hip. "And sex, for that matter. And you know what? Yes. I'm done with fun. You don't get to judge me for that."

I pull away from the table, prepared to leave this place.

Prepared to walk away from the best night I've had in weeks. Months. Maybe years.

Some instinct has me looking back. I glance in time to see Finn push the entire stack of chips, both the ones we started with and the ones I won, to the dealer. "Keep them," he says.

The dealer's eyes light up. "Sir."

Tears prick my eyes. I feel young and naive, even though I know that's ludicrous. Like I really have been sleeping in a forest for a hundred years. And when awakened by Prince Charming, I discovered that he was a billionaire bachelor named Finn Hughes.

When I climb the stairs, there are more people in which to hide.

I plunge into the crowd, hoping he can't catch me.

Maybe I can call an Uber. My driver would be faster, but I don't want anyone catching wind of this. Not my parents. My mother would be thrilled to know I spent the evening with Finn. It's more my overprotective brothers who'd give me shit.

A man stumbles into my path.

For a moment it seems like an accident. I even reach out, as if to help steady him. He seems drunk. Then he turns his eyes on me, full of interest, and I realize it wasn't an accident. He grabs my wrist and pulls me toward the back wall. I fight him, but not hard enough. I'm still shocked this is happening.

"Come on, darling. I'll pay more than the house, and I'll be done faster, too."

It takes me a long moment to realize he thinks I'm a prostitute. Are there house escorts in addition to the cocktail waitresses?

"Let go of me," I say, yanking, panicking.

Then there's a sharp sound, and I'm free.

The man stumbles away, his back hitting the wall. He holds his arm protectively.

Finn is in front of me. "You made a mistake. Apologize."

"Fuck, I'm sorry. I didn't know she was paid for already."

"Apologize to the lady."

Whatever he sees in Finn's eyes makes him flush. "I'm sorry, ma'am."

After a long, tense moment, Finn nods. Men with bald heads and black suits emerge from the crowd and drag the man out the back door. They must have come when they heard a commotion, but they waited for Finn to decide what to do with the man.

Would they have let Finn hurt him?

That's the power of the Hughes name. I shiver.

Finn is handsome and charming, but it would be a mistake to underestimate him.

He turns to me as the crowd returns to their games. "Are you okay?"

"Yes," I say, raising my chin so he believes me. The grip on my forearm will probably leave a bruise. But I have long-sleeved clothes to hide it. Having a childhood like mine made me tough enough to withstand some random asshole.

He takes my arm in his, surprisingly gentle. Two fingers brush along the skin that's screaming in pain right now. It was crushed and twisted in that man's fist. "I should find him and kill him for you."

Another shiver runs through me. "Please. I have enough testosterone to deal with between my father and my brothers."

Finn lifts my arm and lowers his head. He places a featherlight kiss on the place where a yellow-blue bruise will be tomorrow. "I'm sorry I didn't get to you sooner."

My throat closes. A violent man couldn't shake me, but kindness can.

So this is what it feels like to be taken care of.

Strange. Scary. Addictive.

"Time to pack up," someone shouts, and then there's melee.

Finn drags me against his body, shielding me from the crush. The players shove chips into pockets and purses. The dealers slam a lid on the table's banks in what appears to be a practiced move. It's happening so fast I can barely take it in.

"What's happening?" I ask.

The commotion swallows my words, but Finn sees them on my lips. "The cops are coming," he says. "Someone called in a raid. We've got to go."

Chapter Four

Finn

I HALF-CARRY EVA Morelli out the back door.

If she berated me the whole way, I wouldn't blame her. Instead she laughs. It's a wild laugh. A sexy laugh. The kind you make when you're diving off a high cliff.

We're in my car and peeling away from the parking lot as siren lights come into view. Blue and red lights bounce off bricks. They aren't after the patrons. The real goal of these raids is to catch the mysterious Miss M, the woman who owns the underground casino.

It still wouldn't be good to get caught in their net.

Eva Morelli in city lockup? It would be a travesty, but she doesn't look worried. Or pissed that I gave her such a close call. Instead she looks exhilarated.

This.

This is what she'd look like when she's seconds from coming, her cheeks flushed, her eyes sparkling, her hand tight on my arm. I don't know if she even realizes she's still touching me. It's like she's holding on for dear life, and fuck, it feels good.

Then her smile dims. "No one will get hurt, will they?"

Such a caretaker.

If I told her people might get hurt, she'd probably demand I turn the car around.

"Those are some of the wealthiest people in the world. The cops aren't going to risk getting slapped with major lawsuits. They'll be careful if anyone gets caught... which might not even happen. Raids aren't common, but they happen enough that people know the drill."

"Okay." She sits back in the low-slung bucket seat. Her hands go to her cheeks, as if checking that she's still intact. "Okay," she says again.

"Underground gambling. Running from the cops. You're a regular rebel."

She gives a delicate snort. "For two hours, maybe."

"For two hours, so far," I amend. "The night isn't over yet."

One eyebrow rises. "Haven't you ever heard of quitting while you're ahead?"

"That's not how I play, Eva. I'd rather double down."

That earns me an eye roll. "You're such a smooth talker."

"Do you prefer it rough?" I ask, my tone innocent.

She gives me a glare across the stick shift that I assume is supposed to be intimidating. I just find it sexy. I want her to look at me that way while she rides me. I want her to challenge me to make her come while she tries her best not to.

God, victory will be sweet.

Except I'm not going to make her come.

She's not going to ride me.

Not tonight. And probably not ever if she knows what's good for her. It's just as well that she's not known for one-night stands. That way I won't be tempted.

Right, Hughes. Keep telling yourself that.

Eva Morelli isn't the kind of woman you fuck and walk away from.

She's the kind of woman you keep.

And me? I'm a Hughes. Whether we love them or not, we sure as hell leave them.

One way or the other.

It takes her a couple blocks to realize we're heading north instead of east.

Her gaze goes to me. "Your house?"

Something pangs in my heart. My house. She's not asking if she's going to take a tour of the Hughes estate. She's asking whether I'm going to seduce her.

I don't take women to my home.

The idea of Eva there makes my chest feel tight.

"My yacht."

A smile twitches her lips. "Your yacht."

"Surely you've heard of them. Your family owns several."

"Is this how you impress the ladies?"

"I don't need a large boat to impress the ladies. I already have a very large—"

"Thank you, Mr. Hughes. That will be all."

"I was going to say very large jet skis," I say, all innocence. "Though I do appreciate the way you got all hot schoolteacher on me. All prim and commanding. It will be that much more fun when I finally bend you over the desk."

A gasp. And then a laugh. "You *are* a rascal."

"That might be the right word," I admit. "Even if it is a hundred years old."

"Along with rogue."

"Scoundrel."

"Ne'er do well."

"I do certain things very well, actually."

She gives me a reluctant grin. Then her eyes go wide. "That's yours?"

"I told you it was a yacht."

"That's not a yacht. It's a freaking cruise ship."

She exaggerates. A little bit. It's a custom-built superyacht with two pools, a hot tub, a glass bottom, an IMAX theater, and a crew of twenty. They're not here. The boat is quiet on the water as I hand Eva out of the car.

"Not that one," I tell her, leading her past the craft used for events to the fifty-foot bluewater sailing yacht. It's the one I take when I want a long, peaceful ride through the ocean. It also offers some of the best views of the stars in Bishop's Landing.

I climb aboard and then help her make the hop to the deck.

She wobbles a little in my arms, and my hands immediately go around her waist. I steady her in a split second, but I hold her for several heartbeats after that. Her eyelashes brush her cheeks. Demure? Nervous? Then she glances at me, and I see something else entirely.

A fiery passion that's been banked for years.

Heat rushes through my body in implicit

answer.

I force myself to let her go, except for a loose link of our hands. The boat isn't in motion, but it sways gently. I don't want her tumbling overboard. I lead her to the back, where a platform can be used for boarding or sunbathing.

I throw down a couple of outdoor pillows, making us a nest.

Then I pull her down with me.

After an initial stiffness, she relaxes against my side. I'm stretched out flat on the deck, my arm around her. My gaze is on the sky, instead of her, but somehow that makes this moment feel more intimate. I run playful fingertips down her arm, teasing out more goosebumps.

"Beautiful," she says, looking at the stars.

When you lie down like this, you feel insignificant. That's what I like about it. Like I'm a speck of cosmic dust. Like the fate of my entire family, as well as several thousand other families, doesn't rest on my shoulders.

I look down at Eva's face in profile—her strong brow, her faintly upturned nose, her full lips. Her black silky hair tickles my nose. "Beautiful," I murmur in agreement.

Her dark gaze meets mine. "Thank you for tonight."

"For almost getting you arrested?"

"For taking pity on me. I know that's why you did it."

I don't pretend not to understand. "Alex fucking Langley."

She makes a face. "I mean, he's nice. But going to my mom instead of me, the whole arranged-match thing...I hate it. I'm sure you must get that, too."

"Something like that."

There's a ticking clock where I'm concerned.

Get married while you still can, my mother implies with every society chick she introduces me to. I've already told her I'm not getting married.

And I'm sure as hell not having children. Not ever.

I wouldn't do that to them.

"At least he's honest about what he wants. In a way that's better than someone asking me out and charming me as if they want...you know. A real relationship."

"What's wrong with being charming?"

"I don't like charming men," she says, earnest.

It makes me grin. "Everyone likes charming men."

"I want a real relationship with you," I say, my voice low in the style of a confession.

Her eyes are as luminous as the night sky. "Do you?"

The words are hard to get out. "I can't have it."

Because of my family's secrets.

I don't get that with anyone. Especially not a woman like her.

Hurt ricochets through her eyes. She gives a short nod that doesn't quite hide the pain.

I've never been tempted to tell anyone before, but part of me wants to do that now. *It's not you, it's me. It's not you, it's my family. It's not you, it's a modern-day curse.*

"Do you know any of them?" she says, gesturing upward. "The stars?"

"A sailor has to know. That bright spot right there? That isn't a star. That's Jupiter."

She squints.

"And to the right… there's the Lion. And the one right above it, that's Denebola. It's bigger and brighter than the sun. And it's the tail star in Leo. Like your brother."

"Like my brother," she repeats, her words slow and thoughtful. "He's going to have so many questions when my mom tells everyone that I left the gala with you."

"Tell him to mind his own business."

She laughs a little. "No one tells Leo Morelli what to do."

Everyone knows the Morelli brothers are overprotective bastards. Which makes their sisters off-limits unless you're willing to run the gauntlet. I wouldn't let that stop me. I have my own reasons for keeping this casual. "Besides, Sarah Morelli isn't going to tell anyone about one little joyride."

"Oh, she's already told everyone at the gala. I'm sure."

I wince, acknowledging she's probably right. Which means my mother will hear about it. She's no fan of the Morellis, but she's desperate enough to want me married and producing offspring that she'd probably accept it.

"I'll set her straight," Eva says, as if offering reassurance.

As if I'm so intent on bachelorhood that I'd be offended at a rumor. "You know my theory on this. Double down. Convince her we flew to Vegas and eloped."

"Don't," she says, laughing. "She'll start naming our children."

The idea of children makes my smile fade. "Does it matter?"

Eva looks uncertain. "What?"

"What she thinks? Does it matter? Let her believe what she wants."

"Finn."

"I mean it." I lift up on an elbow, resting her head on my forearm. We aren't touching anywhere beneath the belt, but it's still a sexual position. This is how I'd look down at her if I was thrusting inside her, making her moan. I'd lean down and nip her sensitive throat. I'd make her gasp and beg and—No, I won't do any of that. "We can pretend."

"*What?*"

"Let her think we're dating. If she thinks you're already seeing someone, she won't push you to marry Alex fucking Langley. Or anyone else. At least for a while."

"She wouldn't keep it a secret. She'd tell absolutely everyone. Everyone in Bishop's Landing, everyone in New York, maybe everyone in the world."

"So let her. We would know what the truth is."

"But it's not real."

"Who cares what people think? It will get her off your back."

She looks back at the stars. Her profile makes her look regal. Like a queen. "And it would get your parents off your back, too, right? It would work both ways."

"Right," I say, though I don't care as much what my mother says.

Nothing, absolutely no amount of coaxing or browbeating, would ever convince me to marry. It's not just a personal preference. It's a question of ethics. I'd never saddle a woman with someone like me.

Then she turns to look at me. Her expression steals my breath away. She's stunning. She's always looked this way, hasn't she? At balls and galas. At charity dinners. She's always been an untouchable goddess, only I get to touch her right now.

For as long as we're fake dating, I'll get to keep touching her.

"Okay," she says, her tone resolute.

"Okay?"

"I'll pretend to date you."

"Thank God," I say, and then I can't help it. I kiss her. It starts off as a brush of lips. It turns into more. I nibble her full lips, and she opens them on a gasp. A question and answer. A seeking and a solace. She smells so good. I want to inhale her again and again, until my lungs are full, until she pervades every part of my being.

I want to take the kiss deeper. To explore her fully.

Instead I force myself to pull back. "To seal the agreement," I manage in a hoarse voice.

Her lids are still heavy, her dark eyes hazy with pleasure. After a long moment they clear. She searches my expression for something. I don't know what she finds, but it makes her nod.

Then she pulls me down for another kiss. Her lips are soft and welcoming. They promise comfort at the end of a hard day. They feel like poetry written on concrete, incongruous beauty in a harsh, barren landscape. She's the one who takes the kiss deeper. Her tongue darts out, curious. A little playful. And I reward her with a gentle, explicit suck. *This is what I want to do to your clit,* I say with touch instead of words. *You taste so fucking good.*

I'm struck with the thought that I might not be able to stop.

That I might be out here on the deck of my boat for the rest of eternity, kissing Eva Morelli. Even when the sun rises, even when it sets again, even when fall comes, even when the boat sails away for some vacation or other, I might still be here kissing her.

Everyone else can handle their own shit.

It's an absurd notion. I have too much to do. I have responsibilities. My family depends on me. The company depends on me. The secrets definitely depend on me.

And if I waited here long enough, if I kissed her for long enough, she would know.

That is the problem with forever.

I already know how it ends.

Want to read more? Eva and Finn's story ONE FOR THE MONEY is available at Amazon, Apple Books, Barnes & Noble, Kobo, and more bookstores.

About Midnight Dynasty

The warring Morelli and Constantine families have enough bad blood to fill an ocean, and their brand new stories will be told by your favorite dangerous romance authors.

SIGN UP FOR THE NEWSLETTER
www.dangerouspress.com

JOIN THE FACEBOOK GROUP HERE
www.dangerouspress.com/facebook

FOLLOW US ON INSTAGRAM
www.instagram.com/dangerouspress

About Skye Warren

Skye Warren is the New York Times bestselling author of dangerous romance such as the Endgame trilogy. Her books have been featured in Jezebel, Buzzfeed, USA Today Happily Ever After, Glamour, and Elle Magazine. She makes her home in Texas with her loving family, sweet dogs, and evil cat.

Sign up for Skye's newsletter:
www.skyewarren.com/newsletter

Like Skye Warren on Facebook:
facebook.com/skyewarren

Join Skye Warren's Dark Room reader group:
skyewarren.com/darkroom

Follow Skye Warren on Instagram:
instagram.com/skyewarrenbooks

Visit Skye's website for her current booklist:
www.skyewarren.com

Copyright

Made in the USA
Middletown, DE
02 June 2022

66501742R00064